**First published in the United States 1988
by Chronicle Books**

Text copyright © 1987 by Ulf Nilsson
Illustrations copyright © 1987 by Eva Eriksson
All rights reserved. No part of this book may
be reproduced in any form without written
permission from the publisher.
First published in Sweden 1987 by Bonniers
Printed in Denmark
Library of Congress
Cataloging-in-Publication Data

Nilsson, Ulf, 1948-
  [När lilla syster kanin gick alldeles vilse.
English]
  Little Bunny Gets Lost / Ulf Nilsson,
Eva Eriksson.
    p. cm.
  Translation of: När lilla syster kanin gick
alldeles vilse.
  Summary: Little Bunny is happy to be off
on an adventure without her annoying older
brother until she gets lost.
  ISBN 0-87701-530-9 :
  [1. Brothers and sisters—Fiction.
2. Lost children—Fiction. 3. Rabbits—
Fiction.] I. Eriksson, Eva. II. Title.
PZ7.N589Lk 1988
[E]—dc19   88-1042
                                  CIP
Distributed in Canada by   AC
Raincoast Books
112 East Third Avenue
Vancouver, B.C.
V5T 1C8

10 9 8 7 6 5 4 3 2 1

Chronicle Books
San Francisco, California

Little Bunny Gets Lost

Ulf Nilsson ❧ Eva Eriksson

Chronicle Books
San Francisco

One morning Little Bunny set out for a walk all by her very own self.
"Don't go far," warned her big brother.

Little Bunny splish–splashed through every puddle.

She dropped pebbles down a drain. Plip. Plunk. Plip. Plunk.

She crunched through leaves.

She sailed leafy boats.

She skipped stones.

Little Bunny danced.

She twirled. She cartwheeled 'round and 'round.

And when she finished, dizzy Little Bunny had no idea where she was.

The rain began to fall and Little Bunny realized she was lost.

She came to a place that looked very much like her home.
"Perhaps this is where I live," she thought.

But, no, it wasn't Little Bunny's family after all.

"Maybe this is my home," she said.

The newspaper reads:

Woodsy News

Realtors report cozy homes hard to find

But, no, it was the home of sleepy Mr. Badger.

"Maybe *this* is it," she hoped.

But it certainly wasn't! Little Bunny quickly tip-toed away.

She raced through the woods.

The rain began to fall even harder.

Little Bunny thought she was lost forever.

Then, in the distance, she heard a familiar voice.

Big Brother Rabbit had come to find her!
His walk in the woods had made him a bit grumpy.
"I told you not to go so far," he scolded.

But Little Bunny was so happy to see him, she didn't mind.
She even thought that next time,
she just might let him take a walk with her.